the Stable that Bob Built

written by
Cindy Kenney

illustrated by
Greg Hardin · Robert Vann

BIG IDEA
BOOKS®

Zonderkidz

BIG IDEA BOOKS®

www.bigidea.com

Zonder**kidz**®

The children's group of Zondervan

www.zonderkidz.com

The Stable That Bob Built
ISBN: 0-310-70472-3
Copyright © 2004 by Big Idea, Inc
Illustrations copyright © 2004 by Big Idea, Inc.

Requests for information should be addressed to:
Zonderkidz, Grand Rapids, Michigan 49530

Library of Congress Cataloging-in-Publication Data

Kenney, Cindy, 1959-
  The stable that Bob built / by Cindy Kenney.-- 1st ed.
      p. cm.
  Summary: A cumulative rhyme in the style of "The House That Jack
Built" retells the Christmas story, using Bob the tomato and other
Veggies.
  ISBN 0-310-70472-3 (hardcover)
  [1. Christmas--Fiction. 2. Vegetables--Fiction. 3. Stories in rhyme.]
I. Title.
  PZ8.3.K3856St 2004
  [E]--dc22
                              2004000285

Written by: Cindy Kenney
Editors: Cindy Kenney & Amy DeVries
Art Direction: Karen Poth
Illustrations by Greg Hardin and Robert Vann

Printed in China
04 05 06 07/LP/4 3 2 1

/33

straw should be glued to roof (outside)

peak of roof

paint green
same color as
Philippe pea

2-5/16

window top

taller than other side

5'-2 6/12"

window bottom

Knobs
borrow from
Madame Blueberry's
Kitchen. She said it's ok

paint to look
like bricks
on Bumblyburg
Library.

5'-4 2/12

4'-8 1/10

...ks from
...garage.

...of stable, manger and stage in front of stable
...agus we would clean it up after the show)

4'-13 4/21"

paint to look
like a palm tree.
See show #2
for reference

...'s not very big. We just need a place to hang the star and
...e performed at the Bumblyburg Community Theater.

"Do not be afraid. I bring you good news of great joy. It is for all the people.
Today in the town of David a Savior had been born to you. He is Christ the Lord."
Luke 2:10-11

This is
the **stable**
that Bob built.

These are the **lambs**, all cuddly and spry,
that wandered off and followed the **guy**,
who didn't know how to milk the **cow**
that mooed in the **stable** that Bob built.

This is the **shepherd,** who ate apple pie, who cared for his **lambs,** all cuddly and spry, that wandered off and followed the **guy,** who didn't know how to milk the cow that mooed in the **stable** that Bob built.

This is the **angel,** who from on high,
showed the way to the **shepherd** with pie,
who cared for his **lambs,** all cuddly and spry,
that wandered off and followed the **guy,**
who didn't know how to milk the cow
that mooed in the **stable** that Bob built.

This is the **woman**, so young and kind,
that the angel told the shepherd to find.
She showed the way to the **shepherd** with pie,
who cared for his **lambs**, all cuddly and spry,
that wandered off and followed the **guy**,
who didn't know how to milk the cow
that mooed in the **stable** that Bob built.

This is the **man,** who God designed,

to love the woman, so young and kind,

that the **angel** told the **shepherd** to find.

She showed the way to the shepherd with pie,

who cared for his **lambs,** all cuddly and spry,

that wandered off and followed the guy,

who didn't know how to milk the cow

that mooed in the **stable** that Bob built.

This is the **star** that showed the way
for three wise men, who walked all day,
to find the man, who God designed,
to love the **woman,** so young and kind,
that the angel told the shepherd to find.
She showed the way to the shepherd with pie,
who cared for his **lambs,** all cuddly and spry,
that wandered off and followed the **guy,**
who didn't know how to milk the cow
that mooed in the stable that Bob built.

This is the **baby**, the Savior born,

on that very first Christmas morn,

the reason the star had shown the way

for three **wise men**, who walked all day,

to find the man, who God designed,

to love the **woman**, so young and kind,

that the angel told the shepherd to find.

She showed the way to the shepherd with pie,

who cared for his **lambs**, all cuddly and spry,

that wandered off and followed the guy,

who didn't know how to milk the cow

that mooed in the stable that Bob built.

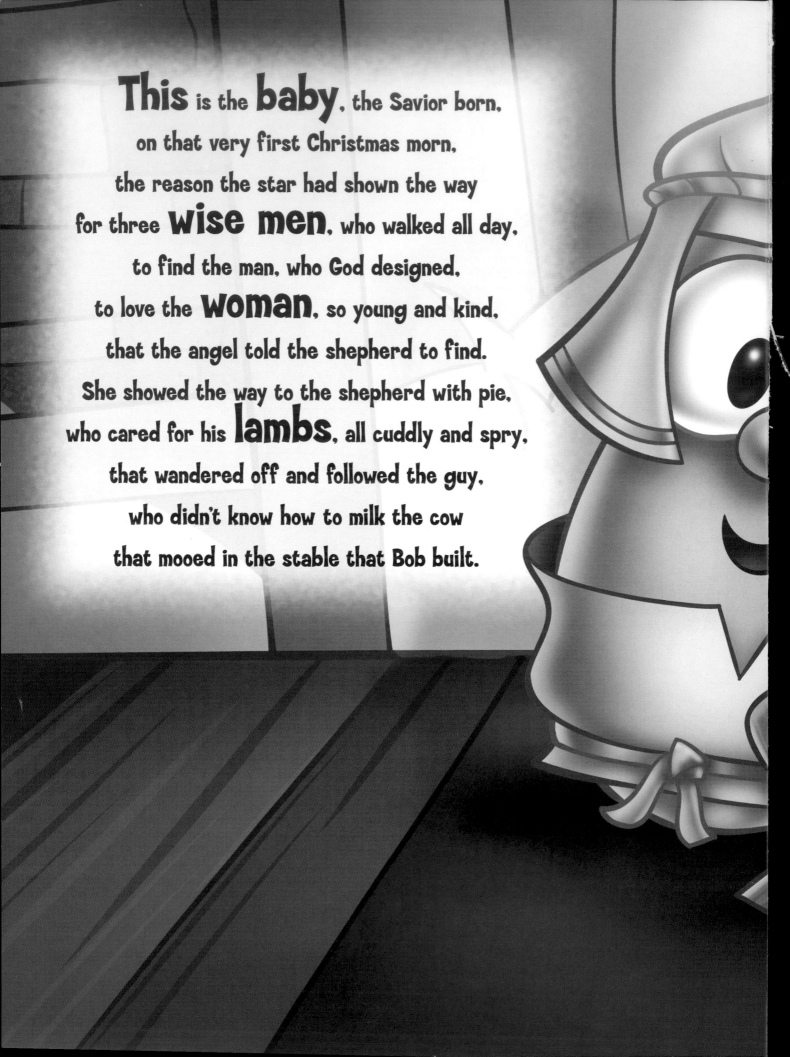

These are the Veggies who played the parts in the story that lives in all of our hearts, to share the news of the Savior born on that very first Christmas morn, all in the Stable that Bob built.

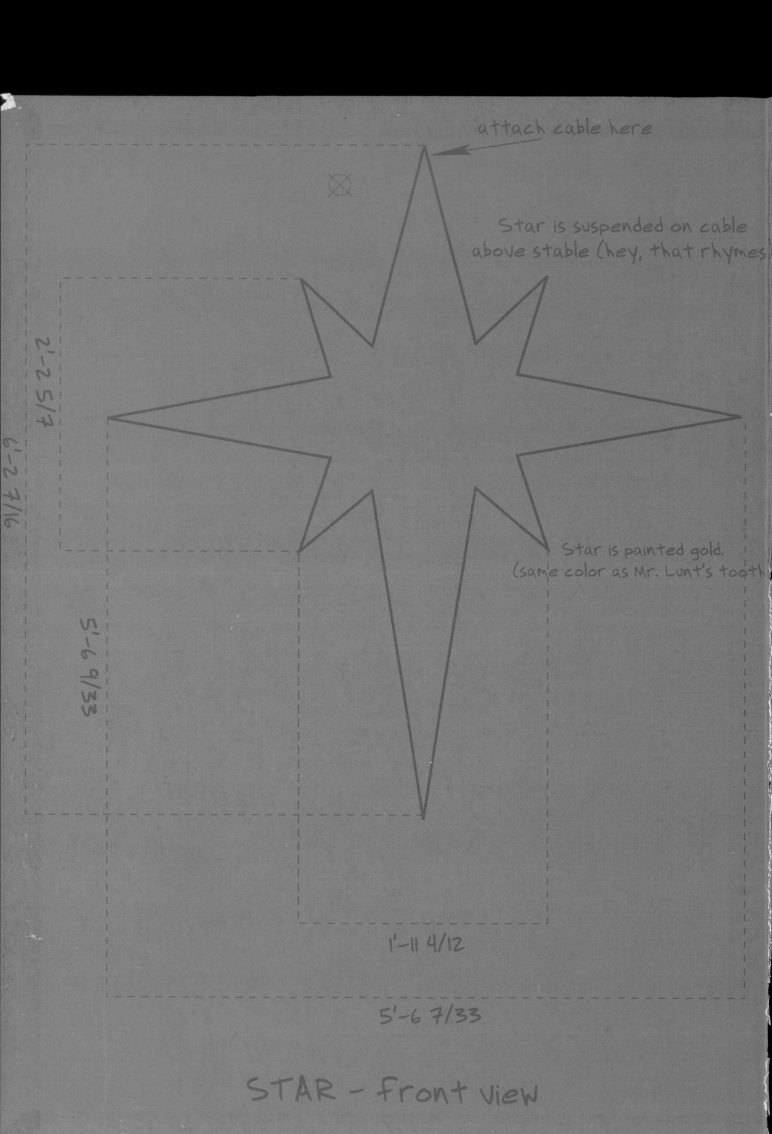

attach cable here

Star is suspended on cable
above stable (hey, that rhymes)

Star is painted gold.
(same color as Mr. Lunt's tooth)

2'-2 5/7

6'-2 7/16

5'-6 9/33

1'-11 4/12

5'-6 7/33

STAR - front view